••

MEG
AND THE
SECRET OF THE
WITCH'S STAIRWAY

••

MEG
AND THE
SECRET OF THE
WITCH'S STAIRWAY

ABOUT THIS BOOK

Lost family silver . . . a family of little old
Civil War dolls . . . riddles written more than
a hundred years ago by Miss Melinda, a little
girl who could not have been unlike Meg and
Kerry . . . a ginger-haired boy who was not,
perhaps, to be trusted . . . a hidden stairway
. . . these added up in Meg's mind to a mystery.
And, oh, how Meg did love a mystery! For
where there was a mystery, she knew, there
must be an answer.

Meg set out to find that answer. Strange, puz-
zling, dangerous, were the events which followed. But Meg did not give up. With her
friend Kerry to help, she kept to her task until
she had unraveled THE SECRET OF THE
WITCH'S STAIRWAY.

Meg

AND THE SECRET OF
THE WITCH'S STAIRWAY

by Holly Beth Walker

illustrated by Cliff Schule
cover illustration by Olindo Giacomini

GOLDEN PRESS
Western Publishing Company, Inc.
Racine, Wisconsin

CONTENTS

1
HIDDEN TREASURE

Gold and *silver* are magic words.

When Meg Duncan's uncle Harold Ashley told about a lost family treasure at the dinner table, Meg's big dark eyes began to glow. Her shiny brown braids swung over her shoulders as she turned toward him.

"Was the treasure worth a lot of money, Uncle Hal?" she asked.

"Yes, it was, Maggie." Uncle Hal looked around at the curious faces turned toward him.

Mr. Duncan, Meg's father, had stopped carving the roast to listen.

Kerry Carmody—a guest at the table and Meg's best friend—dropped a spoon in her excitement.

"The Ashley family silver would be worth a real fortune today," Uncle Hal went on. "But, I'm sorry to say, it disappeared during the Civil War."

"But that was over a hundred years ago!" said Kerry. Her hair was golden in the candlelight. Her small face looked like a surprised pixie's.

Uncle Hal nodded. "That's right, Kerry. I'm glad you know your history. During the Civil War many southern families hid their treasures to keep them safe."

"If the silver is ever found, will it belong to us?" asked Meg eagerly.

"I'm afraid not, Maggie." Uncle Hal smiled at her. "It belonged to a different branch of our family. The silver is said to be buried somewhere on the old Ashley plantation, south of town. As you know,

Miss Jenny and Miss Clara Ashley live there now."

Meg knew the Ashley sisters. They were distant cousins of her mother's. In fact, Meg's middle name was Ashley—Margaret Ashley Duncan.

Miss Clara and Miss Jenny were very old ladies now. The plantation house Uncle Hal was talking about had burned down many years before Meg came to live in Hidden Springs. The sisters now lived in a shabby house near the river. They had a small chicken farm.

"They are fine old ladies," said Meg's father warmly. He put a slice of beef on Kerry's plate. Then he looked at Uncle Hal and chuckled.

"Miss Jenny and Miss Clara are an odd pair, though," he added. "They sell eggs for a living, you know. They drive an old rattletrap of a truck. They are quite a sight, delivering eggs in their white gloves and old-fashioned hats!"

Uncle Hal laughed, too. Then he grew serious. "I'm afraid they are too fond of old-fashioned things," he said. "One day they came into the museum. They wanted to sell an old desk that once belonged to Thomas Jefferson. But when I offered to buy it, they changed their minds. They scooted off in a hurry. I'm sure they are very poor, too."

At those words Meg looked quickly at Kerry. Kerry looked at Meg. Sparks seemed to jump between them.

"Wouldn't it be wonderful if Miss Jenny and Miss Clara could find that lost silver?" cried Kerry.

"Wouldn't it be fun if *we* could find it for them?" said Meg. The thought grew like a bubble inside her, getting bigger and bigger.

Meg and Kerry loved nothing better in the world than a deep, dark mystery. They were fair detectives, too.

"Are there any clues to the hiding place of the silver, Uncle Hal?" Meg asked.

"Yes." He smiled at her. "But don't get your hopes up, Maggie-me-love," he warned. "The Ashley place has been searched a hundred times, I expect. You and Kerry might look pretty foolish, digging up that chicken farm with your little shovels."

"Oh, we wouldn't do that!" Meg was indignant, but she had to laugh at the thought. "We could call on Miss Clara and her sister, though, and ask some questions."

"Let's go tomorrow," said Kerry eagerly. "We were planning on going horseback riding, anyway, Meg."

That was quite true. Kerry's family, the Carmodys, lived not far from the Duncan house, on Old Bridge Road. They had a houseful of children and a yardful of pets, including several horses.

Meg and Kerry often went riding along the stream that cut through the Carmody meadow. They had planned to ride the very next day. But now, with Uncle Hal visiting, Meg hated to go away.

Kerry read her thoughts.

"Why don't you come with us, Mr. Ashley?" she asked eagerly. "You can ride Traveler, my big brother's horse."

"That's a great idea, Kerry," said Uncle Hal. "I might do just that. I think Miss Clara and Miss Jenny would be happy to see us."

Meg felt a glow of pride in her handsome young uncle. He was always ready for any adventure, big or small.

Meg was an only child. Her mother had died when she was a very little girl. Since then, she and Uncle Hal had been the best of pals. Next to her father, she loved him most of all.

"I wish I could join you on this ride," said Mr. Duncan with regret. "But I have to go into town to the office in the morning. And tomorrow afternoon I fly to New York on government business."

Both men worked in the nearby city of Washington, D. C. Uncle Hal worked at a small museum. Meg's father had work with the government.

An elderly couple, Mr. and Mrs. Wilson, looked after Meg and the house in Hidden Springs.

Mrs. Wilson herself came into the dining room just then. She carried a plate of hot biscuits.

She was a gray-haired woman with a kindly face. But she frowned when she looked down at Meg.

"My, oh, my!" she scolded. "You haven't touched a spoonful of your vegetables, Meg. I'm afraid you get too excited when your uncle comes to visit."

"Don't blame me, Mrs. Wilson."

Meg's uncle reached happily for one of the biscuits. "Blame a tale of hidden treasure for Maggie's loss of appetite. She has found a new mystery to chew on."

He was right. Meg was almost too excited now to eat. She wondered if there really was a fortune hidden on the old plantation. Or was it all just another one of the romantic old tales of the Civil War?

"Maybe the silver isn't there at all, Uncle Hal," she said thoughtfully the next day. She was riding at his side through the green Virginia valley on the way to the old Ashley place.

"Maybe not." Uncle Hal bent forward in his saddle to pat Traveler's silky neck. "But Miss Clara and Miss Jenny swear the story is gospel truth. And I have a hunch they're right."

"Why was the family silver hidden, Mr. Ashley?" asked Kerry Carmody. She rode Chappie up to

Traveler's side. Her hair gleamed in the summer sunshine.

"Because the family went away and the silver was too heavy to take," said Meg's uncle.

"The plantation was owned by a man named John Ashley. He was a great-uncle of our two old cousins. He was a proud Virginian, but he hated slavery. He went north to fight with the Yankees."

"And left his family behind?" asked Meg.

"Yes. He had a wife and one little girl named Melinda. He left them in the care of two old, trusted servants. But after he had gone his wife got sick and died. The servants were afraid. They decided to take Melinda to Richmond to her grandmother."

"So they buried the silver," said Kerry.

"Yes. But they never reached the grandmother's house. Nobody ever heard of the servants or little Melinda again. They simply disappeared."

Meg was frowning as she jogged along. "Then how do the sisters know about the silver?" she asked.

"There was a letter found in that old desk," answered her uncle. "The plantation house was empty for many years, for John Ashley was killed in the war. Finally his brother came to live there. He was the grandfather of Miss Clara and Miss Jenny."

"We're almost there!"

As they came around a green hill, Kerry suddenly shouted the words. She touched her heels to Chappie's sides. Then she galloped toward an old two-story house on the hill. Uncle Hal rode behind her.

Meg didn't follow at once. She had stopped, sitting quietly in the saddle. Right in front of her was the place where the first plantation house, the one that had burned, had stood.

The ground was smooth and green, but part of the chimney of an old fireplace still stood. It was covered with vines.

Meg's dark eyes grew wistful. It had been a sad story that Uncle Hal had told. But it could have a happy ending if that lost silver could be found.

She was just about to turn away when all at once something moved near the chimney! A tall,

ginger-haired boy stepped out from behind the bricks. He had a stick in his hand.

He didn't see Meg at first. He began to push the vines aside on the old chimney.

Meg frowned. She started toward him. But at the sound of the hoofbeats, the boy lifted his head.

Then he did a strange thing. He tossed the stick aside and ran toward the riverbank. And suddenly, partway there, he dropped out of sight. He simply disappeared.

Meg rode to the edge of the riverbank. It was high at that spot and she looked down to the stream. She saw no sign of the boy.

Where had he gone?

Then, before she had time to look further, she heard Kerry calling her.

"Come along, Meg!"

Still wondering about the boy, Meg turned and rode up the hill. Kerry and Uncle Hal were already tying their horses to the picket fence at the side of the Ashley house.

2
THE DOLL FAMILY

The Ashley sisters were overjoyed at sight of the visitors. Miss Clara opened the door. Miss Jenny invited them to come in.

"Why, Cousin Hal," they cried together. "What a lovely surprise!"

There were greetings all around. Uncle Hal gave each old lady a happy kiss on the cheek. Then Miss Clara led the way to the parlor. Miss Jenny asked the guests to sit down.

Meg looked around the familiar room with eager dark eyes. The curtains were faded. The rugs were threadbare. But the fine old furniture gleamed with polish as usual.

Then something new caught her eye. A big glass cabinet at one side of the room was filled with tiny, old dolls!

Row after row of little figures, stiffly posed, stared through the glass. Meg stared back in complete delight.

She turned to find Kerry looking in the same direction. The same wonder was on her face.

Uncle Hal was speaking.

"I've been telling the girls about the family mystery," he said with a smile. "Maggie here thinks the story of the hidden silver may be just a legend."

"Oh, it's true, all right," Miss Clara said. She sat up straight in her chair. "Isn't it, Miss Jenny?"

"Yes, indeed," her sister said firmly. "The Ashleys had a famous collection of silver. It was buried right here during the War Between the States.

"Of course," she added sadly, "some of the land

26

has been sold. And the old house burned down years ago. But the silver was never found."

"Maybe it burned up with the house," said Kerry, who had been listening, wide-eyed.

"It couldn't have," said Meg. "Because then they would surely have found it. Metal doesn't burn, Kerry. It would melt into a lump."

"Oh, it wasn't in the house," said Miss Clara. "Grandfather Ashley searched everywhere. He looked for hidden cubbyholes in the attic and for secret places in the cellar. He even dug under all the trees."

"Luckily," put in the other sister, "most of the furniture was saved from the fire." She looked around lovingly. "Why don't we read them the letter from the Jefferson desk, Miss Clara?" she suggested.

Miss Clara jumped up. She opened the big Bible on a corner table. From it she took a folded paper. She handed it to Miss Jenny to read.

Meg sat on the edge of her chair. The letter was surely old. The edges were brown. The paper crackled as Miss Jenny unfolded it.

"This was written over a hundred years ago," she said. "Little Melinda wrote it to her father before the two old servants took her away. But in all the hurry she forgot to send it. And her father never came back. Listen:

" 'My dear, dear Father,

" 'When you receive this I will be in Richmond with Grandmamma. We—Jeb and Nora and I—took the candlesticks and the other silver to the special place, just as you told us to do. Jeb fixed it again so nobody will ever know.

" 'Please, please, Father, make the war be over soon and come for me. I miss my dear mamma and I miss you.

" 'Your loving daughter,

" 'Melinda' "

For a moment the room was quiet. Then Uncle Hal spoke.

"What a sad little letter," he said. "But Miss Melinda speaks in riddles. She didn't tell us where that special hiding place was."

"If only the dolls could talk!" said Miss Clara.

30

She looked at the doll cabinet with its rows of silent watchers. "Perhaps one of those very dolls sat beside little Miss Melinda when she wrote that letter."

"Did they all belong to her?" asked Meg curiously.

"Oh, no." Both sisters rose at once.

"Some of the dolls were Melinda's," said Miss Clara. "But most of them were ours when we were children."

"Our parents traveled a lot," added Miss Jenny. "They brought us dolls from all over the world. They've been in a trunk in the attic until just lately. Would you girls like to see them?"

Would they! In the blink of an eyelash Meg and Kerry were out of their chairs and across the room.

Uncle Hal laughed. "Would puppy dogs like some bones?" he said to nobody. But he, too, came to stand behind them.

Miss Clara opened the cabinet. Miss Jenny took out the dolls.

The first two were exactly alike, except that one had brown hair and one had black. They had leather bodies, painted wax faces, and beautiful

31

blue eyes that opened and closed.

"That was mine," said Miss Clara, pointing to the brown-haired one.

"And that was mine," said Miss Jenny, touching the black-haired doll.

Meg and Kerry saw a world of old dolls. They saw dolls from France and dolls from Germany and a lovely lady from Japan.

They saw a peddler doll that had belonged to Melinda Ashley herself. It was over a hundred years old and wore a calico dress. It had a basketful of wares.

"She has over a hundred and twenty things for sale," said Miss Clara proudly. She held the old-fashioned figure out for her guests to see.

Meg bent with delight over the basket. Never had she seen such tiny things!

There were a miniature pail and a bunch of wee keys. There were a lace handkerchief the size of a stamp and a thimble that would fit neatly over a grain of wheat. There was even another doll, not half an inch tall, with arms and legs that moved.

But of all the dolls, the ones Meg liked best of all stood in a row in the middle of the cabinet—a perfect little family.

There was the father doll. He stood stiff and straight in his old-fashioned clothes. At his side stood his wife in a breathtaking pink satin gown. And between them was their little girl—just eight inches tall.

She had red-brown hair and wide brown eyes, and a sweetly pointed chin. Her dress was white muslin with a blue satin sash.

"That's little Miss Melinda herself," said Miss Jenny softly. "She's wearing the same dress the real Melinda wears in her picture."

Miss Jenny pointed to a painting that hung over the fireplace.

Meg and Kerry turned to look. Yes, there was the same small face, the same glowing hair and brown eyes, and the very dress worn by the doll.

Miss Clara put the dolls away. Miss Jenny closed the cabinet.

"If only the dolls could talk," said Miss Clara

33

once more, "they might tell us where that silver is hidden. Then we could pay the taxes and fix the roof."

"Yes," said her sister, with a little laugh. "That would solve all our problems."

After they had shown their dolls, Miss Clara and Miss Jenny offered their guests lemonade and cookies. Then they showed them around the grounds. They were very proud of their beautiful gardens and fine hens.

The henhouses were very neat.

"I always feed our chickens," said Miss Clara, throwing out some grain.

"I gather all the eggs," said Miss Jenny.

The flower gardens were beautiful. Miss Clara raised camellias: pink, coral, and white. Miss Jenny grew azaleas.

As the guests were admiring the flowers, a little brown dog ran from among the bushes. Its tail was wagging.

"This is Curly," said Miss Clara with a smile. She picked up the little dog and patted him. She put

35

him down again. Right away, Miss Jenny picked the dog up, and *she* gave him a few pats.

At that, Meg looked at her Uncle Hal and grinned. With the Ashley sisters everything was "share and share alike." They even took turns patting the dog!

It was just about then that Meg saw the ginger-haired boy again. She looked past a plum tree and there he was, staring at them from behind a fence.

He threw Meg a sassy little wave. Then he turned and ran off again toward the river.

"Who was that?" Meg cried. She pointed after the running figure.

Miss Clara looked up. "That's Glenn Morgan," she said with a frown. "He's been around the place for a week."

"Wants us to give him a job taking care of the chickens," said Miss Jenny. "But we haven't money to pay him."

"Well, I saw him by the old chimney," said Meg. "And he did something very funny."

She told how the boy had disappeared from sight. Miss Clara laughed. "Must have gone straight down the witch's stairway," she said oddly.

"Yes," said Miss Jenny, who had been listening. "Straight down the witch's stairway!"

Witch's stairway? Before Meg could ask whatever that might be, Uncle Hal spoke. He was looking at his watch.

"It's half past eleven, Maggie," he said. "We'd better get along home. Mrs. Wilson promised me corn bread and gumbo for lunch. She'll be put out if we're late."

3
THE
WITCH'S
STAIRWAY

Meg was quiet on the way back to Hidden Springs. She rode her horse slowly behind Uncle Hal and Kerry, busy with her thoughts.

Who was that strange boy, Glenn Morgan? Why had he come to the Ashley place? What was meant by the "witch's stairway"? And most important of all, where was the hiding place that little Miss Melinda had written about in her letter?

Meg wished that she and Kerry could poke around the old place. The silver must be there somewhere. They might find a clue.

Strangely enough, Meg's wish was to come true. It was to happen even sooner than she had dared to hope.

The next day was Sunday. After church Uncle Hal took her on a long ride in the country. He was an artist and he was teaching Meg to draw and paint, too.

He had a wonderful old Duesenberg car which he had had rebuilt. It was long and low and gleaming black, with red leather seats.

Meg loved to sit beside him, the wind lifting her braids, as the car spun over the highway.

Mrs. Wilson had fixed them a picnic lunch, and Meg and her uncle spent the day in the hills. They hiked. They watched birds. They painted.

Meg was tired and glowing when they came back. She had almost forgotten the Ashley mystery. Then, as they came into the driveway, they saw the sisters' old green truck standing there.

They found Miss Clara inside the house, talking to Mrs. Wilson. Miss Clara was wearing white gloves, and her flowered hat was crooked on her head.

"Oh, Cousin Hal," she cried, at sight of the young man, "something dreadful has happened!"

Meg's uncle took the old lady's hand in his. "Tell me all about it, Miss Clara," he said.

"Miss Jenny has had an accident. *She broke her arm.*" The poor woman was almost crying. Meg felt very sorry for her.

Miss Jenny had climbed on a stool in the pantry. The stool had slipped and she had fallen.

"Luckily for us," added Miss Clara, "that boy Glenn Morgan was nearby. He helped me get Miss Jenny up, and then he ran for the doctor. They took her right to the hospital. She is there now. Oh, Cousin Hal," she wailed, "whatever will I do without Miss Jenny?"

The first thing they did was to visit the patient. They got back into the old Duesenberg. Uncle Hal stopped at the flower shop and bought a bunch of red roses. Then they went to the hospital.

Miss Jenny didn't look very unhappy to Meg. She lay back against the pillows, her arm in a cast. A friendly nurse was fussing over her, and she seemed quite contented.

But when she saw Miss Clara, her face fell.

"Oh, Miss Clara," she cried, "I'm such a goose—breaking my arm like this. Now who will help you do the work? Who will gather the eggs?"

Then Uncle Hal gave her the roses. Meg told her

how sorry she was about the accident. Miss Clara bravely told her not to worry. And when they left her, she was cheerful once more.

"Miss Jenny is right, though, Miss Clara," Meg's uncle said when they were back in the car. "You can't stay alone in that old house and do all the work. I am going to hire somebody to help you."

"No, indeed, Cousin Hal." Miss Clara sat up proudly. She hung onto her hat as they sped down the lane. "I'll get along somehow."

"Shush your pretty mouth, Miss Clara," said Uncle Hal gently. "What are kinfolks for, anyway? To help you when you need them!"

It was then that Meg had her great idea. Wasn't she kin to Miss Jenny, too?

"Why can't Kerry and I do it, Uncle Hal?" she asked. "We'll keep Miss Clara company and help with the work. It will be fun!"

"Why, that's a lovely idea!" said the old lady. "The house needs young folks about."

For a moment Uncle Hal was silent. Meg was afraid he was going to say no. Then he nodded.

"Why not, indeed?" he said. "I'll feel much happier when I go back to Washington if Miss Clara is not alone."

"Of course," he added, "we'll have to talk this plan over with Mrs. Wilson and get permission from Kerry's mother."

That's the way it happened, how Meg Duncan and Kerry Carmody got their chance to explore the old Ashley place.

Of course, they didn't do much "poking around" just at first. There was work to do.

Miss Clara was quite lost without her sister. They had always shared everything. Now Miss Jenny wasn't there to take her turn.

The two girls slept in a big downstairs room next to the library. The first night they lay awake a long time talking—about the accident—about the hidden silver—about the wonderful collection of old dolls.

They finally went to sleep. But hardly had they closed their eyes—or so it seemed—when someone knocked at their door. It was Miss Clara.

"Time to feed the chickens," she said cheerfully.

The two girls rolled sleepily out of bed.

They helped feed the chickens. Then there was breakfast to eat and dishes to do. There was sweeping and dusting, for the sisters were very tidy.

No sooner was all that finished than Miss Clara said, "Now we must gather eggs."

It was fun to gather the warm eggs from under the clucking hens. It was fun to put them in the long boxes.

Meg and Kerry went with Miss Clara in the old green truck to deliver the eggs. After that they went to the hospital to take some flowers to Miss Jenny. And after *that* there were more chores to do.

"No wonder the Ashley sisters never found that hidden treasure," said Kerry wearily that night. She yawned as she crawled into bed. "They have never had time to look!"

Meg laughed as she brushed her long dark hair. She was beginning to see what a big job Mrs. Wilson had, keeping house for her and her father on Culpepper Road.

The next day the work seemed easier. And that

afternoon Meg got another look at Glenn Morgan, the ginger-haired boy. The girls were riding home in the truck with Miss Clara. The boy was walking along the lane. He ran off at sight of them.

That reminded Meg of how he had vanished before.

"What is the witch's stairway, Miss Clara?" she asked curiously.

Miss Clara smiled. "It's just a flight of old stone steps near the river," she said. "Years ago our old washerwoman used to go down the stairway to wash clothes. She reminded us children of a witch when she came back up. The stairway is seldom used now," she added.

"May we see it, Miss Clara?" asked Kerry.

"Why, of course." Miss Clara stopped the truck near the house. "We'll have time to go right now, before we fix supper."

Meg and Kerry ran ahead down the hill, past the old chimney and the great old oak trees. But when they reached the river, they stopped short. They looked around helplessly.

"There it is," said Miss Clara, coming up behind them. She pointed to some bushes, and the girls ran in that direction.

And there it was, behind the bushes, a stone stairway cut into the high bank. The sides were lined with rock, and it was almost hidden from view. Over and through it ran a snarl of twisted vines.

"Oooh! It looks scary," said Kerry, looking down into the dusty tunnel. Then she was off down the steps, bending low to keep the matted vines from catching in her hair.

And Meg was at her heels. One, two, three, four, five, six, seven. She counted the steps as she went. It was indeed a spooky spot.

Halfway down there was a landing about six feet wide.

"Look, Meg!" Kerry pointed to the stone floor. "Somebody's been camping here," she whispered.

Meg moved to take a closer look. She saw a sleeping bag and a bundle of clothes. Lying beside them was a small shovel and a paper sack.

Meg looked in the sack. It contained a box of crackers and three apples. She closed it and put it back beside the sleeping bag.

She looked up, her eyes wide and dark.

"It must be that Morgan boy," she said grimly to Kerry. "What *do* you suppose he's hanging around Miss Clara's place for?"

4

A SOUND
IN THE
NIGHT

When Meg and Kerry came back up the stairway, they told Miss Clara what they had found.

"We think Glenn Morgan is camping down there," said Kerry.

Miss Clara was upset. "That's a dreadful place to sleep. There might be snakes!"

"Then he should go home," said Meg.

"Maybe he doesn't have a home." The old lady

took Meg's arm as they went up the hill. "If you see him again, Meg, tell him I want to talk to him."

Meg saw the boy the very next morning near the chicken pens. He was carrying his shovel over his shoulder.

"Miss Clara wants to see you," she called to him.

"I'll bet she's going to take him in," she added crossly to Kerry, who was petting Curly.

And when they went back to the house, there he was. He was moving his things into a little room behind the kitchen! Miss Clara had set a plate for him at breakfast.

"The poor boy came from Ohio," she whispered. "He has no folks at all. I told him he could stay here till Miss Jenny is well. He was so helpful when she had her accident."

Meg didn't think the plan was wise. And she was sure Uncle Hal wouldn't like it. She didn't trust this strange boy.

Glenn Morgan made himself right at home in the old Ashley house. He ate a huge breakfast of pancakes, sausages, and milk, and as he ate he grinned mischievously over his glass at Meg and Kerry.

But when Miss Clara wanted something, he jumped right up to serve her.

It was *he* who fed the chickens and brought in the eggs after breakfast.

And it was he who rode off in the old truck with Miss Clara to help deliver the fresh eggs to their customers.

"He's up to something," Meg told Kerry darkly. "I saw dirt on that shovel of his. I think he's been digging."

That afternoon Miss Jenny came home from the hospital. And for a time everyone was so busy making her happy there wasn't time to worry.

Glenn moved her chair near a sunny window. Meg and Kerry brought her flowers and pillows. And Miss Clara fluttered about, making tea.

Curly jumped onto Miss Jenny's lap, his tail wagging with joy. He sniffed the plaster cast.

"Why, it's a real celebration!" the old lady said happily.

After supper they all listened while Miss Jenny

told about the hospital. Then Miss Clara played the piano, and Glenn sang folk songs. Meg and Kerry joined in, clapping to the music.

They had such a good time they almost forgot their mistrust of the boy. Then Miss Clara stood up to say good night.

"You can go back home in the morning, girls," she said with a smile. "Now that Glenn is here we'll get along just fine."

Meg could hardly hide her disappointment as she said good night and kissed Miss Jenny's cheek. Then she followed Kerry through the door.

"It's all his fault," said Kerry, when they had gone through the library to their room. "If he wasn't here we could stay around till Miss Jenny's arm is well, I'll bet."

Meg agreed glumly. "Now we won't get to look for the hidden silver."

Meg didn't sleep well that night. She kept dreaming about things in the old house. She dreamed of Melinda, the doll in the glass case.

The doll was trying to talk to her, and Meg

54

couldn't hear through the glass. Then the doll began to twirl, round and round, in her white dress. Suddenly the door flew open. The doll fell to the floor with a *plop*.

Meg woke up. Her eyes were wide open. There *had* been a plopping sound. And it wasn't just a dream. *Someone was in the library.*

Under the door Meg saw a faint yellow glow of light.

She slipped out of bed and pulled her robe around her.

"It's probably Miss Clara," she told herself as she crept to the door. But she had to find out. Carefully she turned the knob and opened the door, just a crack.

Her heart began to pound. It was Glenn! He had a small flashlight and stood near the desk. He was pulling things from a drawer and then throwing them aside.

Meg was more angry than scared. She was just about to burst in on the boy when Kerry woke up with a start.

Frightened at being alone, she cried out, "Meg, where are you?"

At that, Glenn Morgan whirled around. And Meg flung the door open and faced him.

"Just what are you doing in here?" she demanded.

Glenn didn't stay to answer questions. At sight of Meg he turned from the desk. He ran into the hall.

Meg flew after him. But then her foot struck something hard on the carpet. She bent down to pick it up.

It was a small, leather-bound book. She clutched it in her hand as she ran. Down the hall, through the kitchen, after the fleeing boy she ran.

By now, Kerry was at her heels. But when they reached Glenn's room, the door was shut and locked.

Meg pounded on it. "Let me in," she cried. "If you don't, you'll be sorry, Glenn Morgan. Just you wait!"

There wasn't a sound from the room.

"He's a thief," Meg told Kerry. She showed her the book. "He dropped this when he ran. We'd better go upstairs and warn Miss Clara."

They found the old lady sitting up in bed. She was alarmed at seeing the girls.

"What is the matter? Is one of you sick?" she asked.

"No, no," Meg said excitedly. "It's that Glenn Morgan, Miss Clara. I caught him robbing your desk in the library."

For a moment Miss Clara was too shocked to speak. Then she got out of bed and put on her robe and slippers.

"Well, I'll go right down and talk to that young man," she said, her old eyes flashing. "Be quiet," she warned. "We don't want to wake up Miss Jenny."

"And let's hurry," cried Kerry.

Hurry they did. But they were too late. When they reached the little room behind the kitchen, Glenn Morgan had disappeared once more. He was gone—and so were his clothes.

5
A
LITTLE BROWN
BOOK

"He got scared and ran off," said Meg, when they found no sign of the boy. "I'd better call Constable Hosey right away."

Constable Hosey was the law officer in Hidden Springs. He was a good friend of Meg's and Kerry's and had helped them often. But he was surprised to have Meg call him from the Ashley home in the middle of the night.

"You tell Miss Clara not to worry," he said, when Meg told him what had happened. "I'll get right out there and look for that young scamp. Meantime, have Miss Clara make a list of what he stole," he added as he hung up.

By now Miss Jenny was awake. She came downstairs to see what the fuss was about. It took them all to calm her down.

"Glenn seemed like such a nice boy," she said. "All our egg money was in the library!"

They went there at once. A vase had been tipped over. Papers were on the floor. But the egg money was still there—every cent of it!

They checked the silverware in the dining room. It was safe.

Miss Jenny even went back upstairs to see if her pearl ring was in her jewel box. It was.

"Why, he didn't take a single thing!" said Miss Clara.

"Maybe he didn't have time," said Kerry. "Meg scared him off."

"But that egg money was in plain sight," Miss

Jenny reminded her. "I wonder what that boy was after."

It was then that Meg remembered the little book. It was still in her hand. She gave it to Miss Clara.

"Well, he tried to get away with *this*," she said. "I know, because he dropped it when he ran. Maybe it's valuable."

Miss Clara turned the book over in her hands. A puzzled look came over her face. "But this book isn't ours, Meg. I've never seen it before in my life!"

Meg was surprised. She took back the little book and held it under the light. She turned the pages.

"Why, it isn't a real book at all," said Kerry, who was leaning over her shoulder. "It's a diary. There's a date—April second, 1865!"

Meg turned to the front of the book. There, in faded ink, was written a familiar name: *Melinda Ashley*.

"It was *hers*," Meg whispered in awe. "Little Melinda Ashley wrote in this diary. Where do you suppose it came from?"

Both Meg and Kerry were aching to know what

was in the diary. They wanted to sit down at once and try to read the spidery old writing.

But Miss Clara took the little book. She put it in the pocket of her robe.

"We've had enough excitement for the moment," she said firmly. "It's not good for Miss Jenny. I'm going to make us all some nice hot cocoa now. Then we'll go back to bed. In the morning we'll see what it says."

While they were in the kitchen drinking the hot cocoa, there was a knock at the door. It was Constable Hosey. Glenn Morgan was at his side.

"Is this your thief, Miss Clara?" he asked. "I caught him hiking off down the road. But he says he didn't take anything."

The boy wasn't so sure of himself now. He looked sheepish as he faced the Ashley sisters.

"I'm sorry, Miss Jenny, Miss Clara," he said. "I didn't steal anything—honest."

"We know you didn't, Glenn," said Miss Clara.

"But you did break into their things," said Meg accusingly. "I saw you! And you dropped something, too."

The boy hung his head without answering. Then Miss Clara held the little brown book under his nose, and he jerked back in surprise.

He felt anxiously in his pockets. Then he grabbed the diary.

"That's mine," he said. "I must have lost it."

"Who are you, Glenn?" Miss Clara asked. "Why did you come to this house? And where did you get

a diary that belonged to Melinda Ashley?"

The boy looked boldly around at the questioning faces.

"Melinda Ashley was my great-grandmother," he said at last. "My father gave me this book before he died. It tells all about this old plantation and how to find it. Maybe you don't know it, but a fortune in silver was hidden on this place. I came to find that silver, if it's still here."

"What makes you think you will find it?" Meg demanded. "Nobody else can."

Glenn held up the diary. "Because this little book tells where it is. That's why I went into the library tonight. I thought there might be a map of the old plantation. I think the silver is buried somewhere near a hidden spring. All I have to do is find the spot."

"You've already been digging around here," said Kerry flatly. "We saw you with that shovel."

The boy looked embarrassed.

"You had no right to do that, young fellow," said Constable Hosey. "This land belongs to Miss Clara and Miss Jenny now."

"But he's kinfolk to us, Constable Hosey!" Miss Jenny was all in a tizzy. Her eyes were snapping. "Why, his great-grandmother, Miss Melinda, was niece to our own grandfather. He's more than welcome here, isn't he, Miss Clara?"

Miss Clara didn't answer. But she looked kindly at the boy. She poured two more cups of cocoa and set out a plate of cookies.

"Sit down, Constable," she invited. "You, too, Glenn. This has been an exciting night. We'll talk about it tomorrow."

Meg frowned at the boy over the rim of her cup. She still wasn't sure that she quite trusted him. How she wished that she and Kerry could have a good look at that little brown book!

6

CURLY FINDS
A BONE

Nothing was said the next morning about going home, and so Meg and Kerry helped with the work as usual.

Of course at breakfast the talk was all about Melinda Ashley and the treasure. Glenn wouldn't let anybody touch his precious diary. But he told them what was in it.

"She wrote about the Civil War and what happened after," he said. "Melinda was eleven years old when she left this place. Two old servants tried to take her to Richmond, but the Union soldiers wouldn't let them go that way. So they went north. When they got to Ohio they were caught in a mob of people. Melinda lost sight of Jeb and Nora. She never could find them again."

"Poor little thing," said Miss Jenny sadly.

"Then what happened?" begged Kerry.

"A kind family took her in, finally. Their name was Morgan, the same as mine. When she grew up she married one of the sons."

"Why didn't she ever come back?" asked Meg.

"The family was poor," he answered. "People didn't travel so much in those days. Besides, Melinda did try to reach her father. She wrote, but he never answered."

"He couldn't," put in Miss Clara. "He never came back to this house. After she left no one lived here for over twenty years!"

"Anyway," Glenn went on, "when she grew up she worried about that silver. The Morgans didn't

believe her story. She talked fancy and was always
making up riddles. It was a kind of game. But I read
her diary real good," he added. "I think the silver
is buried around here. And I aim to find it."

"What makes you think it's near a hidden spring?"
asked Meg. She stood up to clear the table. She
longed to get her hands on that little diary.

Glenn pulled it from his pocket. "Because it says

so right here. She wrote it in a kind of poem. 'Paul Revere won't ride again,'" he read, "'till you find the hidden door.'"

He looked at the others. "The diary says some of the silver was made during the Revolutionary War. Paul Revere was a silversmith. I learned that in school."

Meg looked at the boy with new respect. "That's

clever thinking, Glenn," she told him. "That means the silver can't be moved till you find the hiding place! Go on, Glenn."

"There's some more stuff that doesn't mean anything. Then it says, 'A hidden spring comes into play.' "

"That isn't a very good clue!" said Kerry in disgust.

"It might be." Miss Clara looked thoughtful. "There used to be a lot of little springs around here. The town was named Hidden Springs."

"There was one on this very land," said Miss Jenny. "It's all dried up now and grown over with berry bushes."

By now Meg was excited again. "That must be it," she cried. "Where is the spring, Miss Jenny?"

"Over the little hill behind the henhouses."

Meg, Kerry, and Glenn were all on their feet.

"Do you mind if we dig around there?" Glenn asked eagerly.

"Not at all," said Miss Jenny.

Miss Clara promptly added, "Just as soon as we

deliver the eggs, you may dig all you like. It would be wonderful if we found that silver after all these years. Wouldn't it, Miss Jenny?"

"Oh, yes!" Miss Jenny was terribly excited. "It's nice to find we have a new cousin, too." She beamed at Glenn.

Digging was hard work. Bushes were matted around the rocks at the site of the old spring.

Glenn chopped the bushes away with an ax. With the help of the two girls he pushed the stones aside.

"There's supposed to be a hidden door," he said as they started to dig.

They found no door. The three treasure hunters dug until their hands were sore and their backs ached. Then they dug some more.

Curly, the friendly little brown-haired dog, tried to help. He kept getting in the way, making the dirt fly in their faces. Meg was glad when a squirrel ran by. Curly saw it and chased it toward the river.

"It's no use." At last Kerry threw down her shovel. "There's no treasure here, Glenn."

The boy looked woeful, but stubborn. "There must be another spring," he said.

Just then the little dog came running back up the hill. He ran across Meg's feet with something in his mouth.

Meg wondered what it was. "Bring it here, Curly," she called.

When he didn't obey she started after him. He flew toward the river and down the witch's stairway with Meg behind him.

She counted the steps as she always did. One. Two. Three. Four. At the seventh step poor Curly stumbled. He went sliding on his nose. He dropped his plaything.

Meg had to laugh as she caught up with him. But she felt sorry for him, too. She sat down on the landing in the middle of the stairway and called to him.

"Here, Curly." She patted her knee.

The little dog came whimpering to her to be patted. Then she saw the thing he had dropped. Gently she pushed him aside to pick it up.

It was a small fork. She had never seen one like it. It had three metal prongs and a bone handle. Curly had been chewing on the handle.

Meg turned the fork over. It looked old, she thought, like something out of a museum. Where had it come from?

Sitting in that spooky place, Meg shivered. A little wind brushed her cheek like a cold finger. Suddenly she had a feeling that someone was looking down at her!

She pushed the fork into her pocket, along with the small sketch pad and pencil she always carried. Then she jumped to her feet and started back up the stairway.

She stopped in her tracks. Someone *was* watching her. It was an old woman in a weird hat. Scraggly gray hair blew around her face.

For a moment Meg thought she was seeing a witch!

The woman glared at Meg from the top of the stairway. Then she turned quickly and hurried from sight.

7
AN ANCIENT RIDDLE

When Meg came up from the stairway, the strange woman was near the old chimney. She must have been there before, Meg thought. But Meg had been so busy chasing Curly she hadn't seen her.

When the woman saw Meg again, she went up the hill to the road. A car was parked there. She climbed into it.

Puzzled, Meg followed. At the brick chimney she

stopped. Someone had pulled the vines from the fireplace wall! A brick had fallen out. There was a dark hollow where it had been.

As Meg stood there, watching the car drive away, Kerry and Glenn came up. They had put down their shovels.

"There's no treasure buried near that old dry spring," said Kerry flatly. "Glenn was following a red herring for sure. A red herring—that's a false clue," she told him.

"I guess you're right, Kerry." The boy wiped his forehead with his sleeve.

"But something queer happened after you went off," he said to Meg. "Two cars drove up by the fence near where we were digging. Some men got out and walked down to the river."

"There was somebody here, too," said Meg. She told them about the mysterious woman she had seen. "I wonder why people are prowling around here all of a sudden."

When they went back to the house they learned the answer. Miss Jenny had been busy that morning

while everyone else was working.

She had phoned the newspapers. She had called the radio station. She just had to spread the wonderful news—that the Ashley family had found a new cousin.

"You shouldn't have done it, Miss Jenny," said her sister sternly. "Half the people in Hidden Springs have called on the phone wanting to find out about Glenn and that diary of Melinda's."

Miss Jenny looked guilty, but stubborn. "I didn't mean to tell about the silver," she admitted. "But those reporter people ask so many questions. Anyway, I'm proud that Glenn Morgan is a cousin of ours!"

"So am I." Miss Clara looked at the tall boy who stood nearby with the two girls.

They were all in the kitchen helping her prepare supper. "But I don't want people prowling around our land looking for treasure!"

"They already are," said Meg suddenly. She told about what had happened when she chased Curly down the witch's stairway.

That reminded her of the strange little fork. She pulled it from her pocket and handed it to Miss Clara.

"Curly dug this up from somewhere."

Miss Clara frowned. "I've never seen that before, Meg. But it does look awfully old. Why don't you call Cousin Hal at the museum and describe it to him? He knows all about old things."

So Meg did just that.

Uncle Hal got quite excited when she described the little fork.

"It sounds like a piece of old-fashioned tableware, Maggie. It might even be from that lost Ashley collection."

"But it isn't made of silver, Uncle Hal."

"No, but it is the type of fork people ate with during Revolutionary times. I'm driving to Hidden Springs tonight," he added. "I want to bring a present to Miss Jenny. And I want to see that fork!"

He was even more excited when Meg showed it to him later.

"It's certainly very old," he said. "The dog must

have dug it up from around here somewhere. Maybe he found it near the old spring where you were digging."

In answer to her uncle, Meg shook her dark braids.

"He brought it from somewhere near the river, Uncle Hal. We didn't dig up anything interesting near the old spring."

"Well, if we don't find that hidden silver soon," said Kerry, "somebody else will beat us to it. Now that people in Hidden Springs know about it they'll all be coming out here and digging all over the place!"

At that, Meg turned to face Glenn. "Give me the diary," she pleaded. "Maybe *I* can find out something from reading it."

Slowly Glenn took the diary from his pocket. He opened it and held it out for her to read. "It tells right there about the hidden spring. Melinda wrote riddles all the time. It was a game she had with her father. She wrote about where she hid the silver in that poem. You can read it."

Meg wasted no more time. She grabbed the diary from Glenn and read the poem aloud to the rest of them.

> " 'Paul Revere will ride no more
> Until you find the secret door;
> When Monticello points the way,
> A hidden spring comes into play.
> A secret within a secret see—
> Mrs. Manythings has the key!' "

"That's a real riddle, all right," said Kerry in awe. She was standing near the parlor window. "But what does it mean?"

Meg was frowning over the strange words.

"Well, *Paul Revere* must stand for the silver," she said. "Glenn was right about that. We can't move the silver till we find that secret door. But—*Monticello points the way. . . .*"

Meg began to laugh. She looked up at the boy. "Glenn Morgan," she cried, "don't you know what *Monticello* is?"

"I never heard of it."

"Why, it's Thomas Jefferson's famous home near

Charlottesville," said Kerry in disgust. "Every kid in Virginia knows that. There's even a picture of it on our five-cent piece."

Uncle Hal took a nickel from his pocket. Without a word he handed it to poor Glenn.

"And *Monticello* must stand for that old Jefferson desk you told us about, Miss Clara." Meg was terribly excited now. She faced the two old sisters. "The clue to the hiding place of the silver must be in that old desk!"

Before either sister could answer, Glenn spoke up. "Then the *hidden spring* isn't in the ground at all," he shouted. "It opens a secret drawer in that old desk!"

His ginger-brown head bent beside Meg's as they both studied the riddle. " 'A secret within a secret see,' " he read. "That could just mean there is a secret place inside a secret drawer. And 'Mrs. Manythings has the key—' "

"That's a big help," said Kerry gloomily. "Mrs. Manythings—whoever she was—is probably dead and gone long ago."

"Maybe not." Meg's big dark eyes were thoughtful. All at once they began to glow. "Miss Clara—Miss Jenny, may I open the doll case?"

They looked surprised. "Why, of course, Meg," said Miss Clara.

Before the words were out Meg was running to the glass case. She came back carrying the funny old peddler doll that had belonged to Miss Melinda.

"Here is your Mrs. Manythings, Kerry," she said. "Melinda gave her the key to keep." From the peddler's basket she took the ring with its tiny keys.

Happily she held them up.

"I think you have the answer, Maggie." Uncle Hal smiled proudly at his niece. "Melinda must have left a message for her father in the old desk in case he didn't get the letter she wrote. Now the big question is"—he faced the Ashley sisters—"where is the Jefferson desk?"

For a moment there was silence. An odd look passed between the two sisters.

"It's upstairs in my room," said Miss Clara firmly.

"In *my* room," said Miss Jenny, just as surely.

8
THE JEFFERSON DESK

"Come with me," said Miss Clara. "I'll show you the desk."

There was a wide hall at the top of the stairway. Miss Jenny's room was on the left. Miss Clara's was on the right.

Miss Clara opened her door. "There it is," she said proudly, pointing. "That is the Jefferson desk. We believe that it once stood in Monticello."

It was a beautiful desk made of walnut. It had several rows of tiny doors and drawers.

Meg and Kerry flew toward it.

"May we look inside?" Meg asked.

Miss Clara smiled. "You don't need to look," she said. "I'll show you the secret drawer myself. We've known about it all along."

She took out one of the small drawers. Behind it was another drawer. She pressed a hidden spring and out came the second drawer.

"There it is, Meg. But there is no clue there, as you can see. It's full of old recipes." She emptied them out onto the desk.

Kerry sighed with disappointment. But Meg wasn't satisfied.

"The riddle said a secret *within* a secret," she said. "Maybe this drawer has a false bottom."

By now Glenn had the tiny drawer in his own hands. He and Uncle Hal looked it over carefully. They even measured the bottom and sides.

"No luck," said Glenn at last.

Then they looked at all the other drawers. They

knocked on the legs of the desk to see if they were hollow. But they found no "secret within a secret."

All this time Uncle Hal's face was growing more and more serious.

"Miss Clara," he said at last, "I have bad news for you. This desk never belonged to Thomas Jefferson. It isn't even very old. It's just a very good reproduction."

At that, Miss Clara's face turned white. But Miss Jenny, who had been standing primly by all this time, gave a squeal of delight.

"Then my desk is the real one," she cried.

"Are there two desks?" gasped Meg. Then she remembered—Miss Jenny had said the desk was in her room.

"Yes," said Miss Clara sadly as they all followed her sister across the hall. "There are two desks. Miss Jenny and I always had everything just alike. We both wanted to own the Jefferson desk. So our mother had a cabinetmaker copy the desk. The two look exactly alike. But I always thought mine was the real one."

"There is the real one," said Miss Jenny. She pointed proudly to the second desk, in her room.

To Meg, it looked exactly like the desk that stood in Miss Clara's room. There were even the same scratches on the front.

The secret drawer in Miss Jenny's desk was full of old love letters. She blushed as she took them out.

Again they looked anxiously for the "secret within a secret." And again they found no clue in the old desk to the hiding place of the Ashley silver.

Uncle Hal pulled the desk out and looked closely at the back of it.

"There's something fishy here," he said. "I'm sorry to tell you this, Miss Jenny, but your desk is a fake, too. A very clever piece of work."

The two old sisters were too shocked to speak.

"Then where is the real Jefferson desk?" asked Meg in dismay.

"I don't know," said her uncle, "but I think we'd better find that old cabinetmaker." He turned to the sisters. "Do you know where to find him?"

"Oh, I'm sure he must be dead by now," said Miss

Clara. She frowned thoughtfully. "His name was Turner," she said after a time. "Andrew Turner. He and his daughter moved away from Hidden Springs many years ago. I think they went to Washington."

"Well, if he worked in Washington the museum may have his address," said Uncle Hal. "We hire fine carpenters to repair old furniture. I'm going back to the capital in the morning. I'll try to trace him. We still may find the Jefferson desk."

"Oh, may we go with you?" asked Meg eagerly. "Now that Glenn is here, Miss Clara and Miss Jenny don't need us anymore."

"Please, Mr. Ashley." Fair-haired Kerry echoed Meg's wish.

Uncle Hal smiled down at the two young faces. "I don't see why not, if it is all right with Mrs. Wilson and your mother, Kerry. Get your suitcases and I'll take you home now."

A trip to the nation's capital was always a big adventure for Meg and Kerry. They felt very important the next morning as they whisked along the highway in Uncle Hal's long, black car.

They were dressed exactly alike in red and blue outfits. In her small, white purse Meg had the ring

of tiny keys which had been in Mrs. Manythings' basket.

It wasn't long before they saw the gleaming white shaft of the Washington National Monument against the blue summer sky.

The first thing they did when they got to the city was to go to the museum where Meg's uncle worked.

It was just a small museum. But it was filled with wonderful things. Uncle Hal proudly showed them a cabinet full of very old silver and gold tableware— pitchers and candlesticks and bowls.

"Here is a pitcher made by Paul Revere himself," he said.

He put it in Meg's hands. It was very plain. But it was heavy and shining.

"It's worth a lot of money, just because the great American patriot made it," said her uncle. "Paul Revere was also a goldsmith."

"I hope we find some gold things, too, when we find the hiding place of the Ashley silver," said Kerry fervently.

"*If* we find the hiding place," said sensible Meg.

After that, Uncle Hal led them up a narrow stairway to the funny little office where he worked. He looked in a lot of old notebooks and papers for Andrew Turner's address. Luckily he found it.

"Just as I thought," he said. "The museum used to hire him to fix old furniture. I hope we can find somebody who knows what happened to that Jefferson desk."

Uncle Hal told his secretary that he would be back after lunch, and away they went again.

They found the address without any trouble. It was on an old street outside of the city, a very small cottage at the back of a weed-grown lot.

At first Meg thought nobody was home. The house looked closed and neglected. But when they rang the bell the door opened, just a crack.

"What do you want?" asked an unfriendly voice through the narrow opening.

"Is this where Mr. Turner used to live?" asked Uncle Hal, from behind Meg's head.

"Yes, it is," the voice said sharply. "But he's dead

—died long ago. I'm Beulah Turner, his daughter."

To Meg's dismay, the door started to close.

Uncle Hal put his hand against it. "May we come in, Miss Turner?" he asked politely.

"What for?"

The door opened wide, and Meg got the surprise of her life.

She found herself face to face with the woman she had seen the day before near the witch's stairway. The woman's hair hung wild around her face. She stared at her three visitors out of beady, suspicious eyes.

It was clear that the woman wanted them to go away. But Uncle Hal was smiling. And when that young man smiled it was very hard to refuse him anything.

9

A SECRET
WITHIN
A SECRET

Before Meg quite knew what was happening, they were inside the little house.

And there—right in front of her eyes—was the Jefferson desk.

It looked exactly like the other two. But Meg had a spooky feeling about this one. *It had to be the real one.* She could hardly wait to look inside.

"That's a fine old desk," said Uncle Hal. He

walked toward it with Meg and Kerry at his heels. "I'm Harold Ashley from the museum. I'm interested in buying old furniture."

"It ain't for sale," said Beulah Turner. "That desk belonged to my father. It's mine now."

"Are you sure about that?" Uncle Hal ran his hand over the fine old wood. Then he turned to face the woman.

He looked her straight in the eye. "Didn't this desk come out of the Ashley home at Hidden Springs?" he asked.

"No, no!" The woman twisted her hands together.

"I think it did," said Uncle Hal sternly. "Andrew Turner was hired to make a copy of a valuable desk for the owner. Instead of that, he made two copies. He kept the real one for himself."

He turned back to the desk. "There's a secret drawer in here, Miss Turner. Did you know that?"

The woman shook her head. But she looked scared now. And she didn't do a thing when Meg's uncle opened the desk. He took out the little hidden drawer.

"This is it, Meg." He smiled as he handed it to her. "It looks like the others, but it's not quite the same. Can you see the difference?"

Meg studied it carefully. Her heart sprang to her throat.

"It isn't deep enough," she whispered. "It has a false bottom. That means there is a hiding place underneath. If we can only open it—"

It was Kerry who stuck out a pink finger to push aside a wooden button. And there was a tiny keyhole!

Meg's fingers shook as she opened her purse. She tried the tiny keys, one by one. The very last one fitted the lock. As she turned it, the back of the drawer fell away.

There was a second little drawer—the "secret within a secret" of Melinda's diary.

"Hurry, Meg!" Kerry was breathing down Meg's neck. "See what's inside!"

Meg pulled out the tiny drawer. It was empty.

Both girls groaned in disappointment.

"Miss Turner," Uncle Hal said, "someone opened this drawer without the key. How was it done?"

The woman backed away. "My father found that hiding place. He didn't want to break the lock, so he took the back from the drawer, then put it back together again."

"And he took something out of the drawer. A paper of some kind."

"Yes, there was a paper there," she admitted. "It had an old poem on it. I threw it away!"

Meg knew she was lying.

"That paper belongs to the Ashley sisters," Uncle

Hal said. "It's important. I suggest that you give it to me."

"*It belongs to me!*"

The woman's face was stubborn. "I didn't know it was important at first. It just has a silly poem on it. Then I heard on the radio about that Morgan boy being in Hidden Springs looking for buried treasure. That paper tells where it is. Buried treasure belongs to anybody who finds it—"

"You were at the Ashley farm yesterday, weren't you?" said Meg. "I saw you there near the old chimney."

"I was just looking around," the woman said slyly.

Uncle Hal was getting impatient. "Give us that paper, Miss Turner. It will save you a lot of trouble if you do. You must know by now that Andrew Turner stole this desk."

At those words the woman seemed to shrink. Meg felt almost sorry for her.

"It's true," she said. "My father loved old furniture. He kept the real Jefferson desk and gave the

Ashley family the two fakes. He thought they'd never know the difference."

"The *paper*, Miss Turner."

She went out of the room. When she came back she gave Meg's uncle a folded piece of yellowed paper. "Doesn't make much sense," she said.

Uncle Hal put the paper in Meg's hands.

"Keep it safe, Maggie," he told her. "It may be the clue you and Kerry are looking for.

"As for the desk," he said to Miss Turner, "you know very well that it is a priceless treasure. It does not belong to you. I hope that the Ashley sisters will see fit to put it in the museum."

Meg opened the folded paper. There was writing on it. Slowly she read the faded words aloud:

" 'To see the silver gleam again,

You must work with might and main;

Seven up and seven down;

Make the wall come tumbling round.' "

Kerry's small pixie face was a picture of disappointment. "It's just another old riddle! It doesn't tell us where to look at all!"

Uncle Hal didn't speak until they were in the car. "I agree," he said then. "And I'm too hungry to guess at riddles. We'll go to my apartment and wash up. Then I'll treat you charming young ladies to a fancy lunch in the city. Now, what do you think about that?"

Uncle Hal lived alone. His apartment was full of paintings he had done. Meg and Kerry looked at them while he put on a fresh shirt. Then they went downtown to a big restaurant in the heart of Washington, where they were served with much flourish by a French waiter.

The lunch was super-special. But between every bite Meg and Kerry jabbered about the curious riddle. They read it over a dozen times trying to make sense of it.

" 'Make the wall come tumbling round.' What wall?" Meg squeezed her eyes shut. She remembered a wall with one brick missing. And the dark hollow behind it.

Her dark eyes flew open again. "Why, it must be in the old chimney," she cried.

"But 'seven up and seven down'—what does that mean?" asked Kerry.

Meg was excited now. "That could stand for the rows of bricks. I'll bet there are that many rows in the wide part of the fireplace. Remember that letter Melinda wrote to her father? She said Jeb fixed the special place so no one would ever know. Maybe he took out some of the bricks and hid the silver, then put them back again—"

"You may be right, Maggie," said Uncle Hal, nodding. "There is room for a hiding place between the chimney wall and the firebox. I wish I could go back to Hidden Springs with you right now and help you look. But I can't. I have to get back to the museum."

"Don't worry, we'll call you up and tell you if the silver is there, Mr. Ashley," promised Kerry when he put them on the bus for home late that afternoon.

"Be sure to keep your fingers crossed, Uncle Hal," said Meg.

10
SEVEN UP
AND
SEVEN DOWN

"Meg is right," said Glenn the next morning. "That silver must be in the old chimney!"

Meg and Kerry had come on horseback to the farm right after breakfast. They were in the kitchen now. They had already told Miss Clara and Miss Jenny about how they had found the Jefferson desk in Washington.

Meg read Melinda's riddle to them.

"Do you mind if we tear down the old chimney?" she asked eagerly.

"Of course not," said Miss Clara. "As soon as Glenn and I deliver the eggs you can get at it."

"It's an eyesore, anyway," put in Miss Jenny. Her cheeks were flushed with excitement.

The task wasn't going to be an easy one. Meg found that out later when, after Glenn and Miss Clara returned from town, they examined the old chimney. It looked solid. The bricks were big. But— there were fifteen rows of bricks in the widest part.

Meg counted with growing excitement. "Seven above and seven below!"

Glenn brought tools and a stepladder. He climbed up and hammered the bricks out, one by one. He handed them to the girls. They piled them nearby.

It was hard work. At noon, Miss Clara brought them cold milk and sandwiches. But she hurried away again, leaving them to their work.

"Miss Jenny isn't feeling well. She's had too much excitement. The doctor told her to lie down."

Little by little the wall came down. But it was

all for nothing. There was a space behind the fire-place, but there was no sign of the silver.

The only treasure they found was a broken wooden doll, tossed there by some child long ago.

At last they gave up. Glenn threw down his tools in disgust.

Meg sat beside Kerry on the pile of bricks. She was tired. Her face was streaked with dirt and sweat. She stared toward the riverbank, so disappointed she wanted to cry.

"A lot of good that dumb riddle did us," said Kerry darkly. " 'Seven up and seven down'—phooey!"

Meg didn't answer. But the words went around and around inside her head.

Just then Curly dashed down the hill, barking with all his might. He ran toward the witch's stairway. At the same time, a little breeze blew up from the river, touching Meg's wet cheek. It was like an icy slap to her senses.

Meg jumped to her feet. Without a word to the others she flew toward the stairway and down the steps. Her heart was beating like a wild thing.

One, two, three, four, five, six, *seven!* Seven steps to the stone landing. Down she went to the river, seven more steps. *Seven up and seven down.* Why, that was it!

Meg raced back to the center of the stairway. She stared at the rock wall. There was a tiny hole in the cement between the rocks. She put her finger to it. A little cold breeze flowed from the hole.

By now, Kerry and Glenn were beside her.

"What's the matter?" asked Kerry.

"I've found it!" Meg could hardly talk. "There are fourteen steps in the witch's stairway, seven up and seven down. There must be an old cool cellar behind this wall."

"I believe you're right." Glenn bent down to study the mossy rockwork. "It looks as if a square opening had been filled in here. Kerry," he said, "bring me a little stick."

Kerry found the stick and Glenn pushed it through the hole between the rocks. It hit something. He pushed harder and the stick went through.

114

"There's wood back there," he shouted. "It's rotted out. That must be the hidden door!"

"But how are we going to get to it?" asked Meg. "That rock wall will be harder to tear down than the chimney!"

The boy's eyes narrowed. "Maybe we won't have to take out the rocks," he said. "There's air coming through this hole. That means the cellar has another opening. Let's look near the bottom of the stairs and see if we can find it."

All three were soon down the steps, searching the bank at the edge of the river.

"See, Meg." Kerry bent over, looking at the ground. "Here are some of Curly's paw prints."

She followed the tracks. They led around a clump of bushes and halfway up the steep bank. There was an opening in the hillside. It wasn't very big, but the little dog tracks went right on into it.

"Why, that's where he got the bone-handled fork!" Meg cried. "He ran up from the river with it. The Ashley silver must be back in there."

The little dog came running up from behind her

just then. She picked him up and patted him.

"What do we do now?" asked Kerry.

"We dig," said Glenn Morgan. The tall boy had taken charge. "It can't be far back to that old cellar. It will be easier to dig a tunnel from here than to tear down the wall. Let's get the shovels."

They decided not to tell Miss Clara and Miss Jenny about their latest find.

"They'd just get all excited again," said Meg. "And maybe we won't find the silver after all."

Glenn did most of the digging, but the girls took turns, too. The earth was damp and the work went fast. Glenn decided to make the tunnel just big enough to crawl through.

Meg never did remember how long it took. But the sun was low in the sky when Glenn made a thrilling discovery.

His head was in the tunnel. His feet were sticking out. Meg could just hear his muffled shout.

"I've reached it! It's a room, all right. The sides are boarded up. But the wood is so rotten, animals have already made holes in it."

Then he backed out with his flashlight and stood up. His clothes were soiled. His grinning face was smeared with dirt.

"There's a bunch of stuff in there, all right," he said. "I couldn't see what it was because I have to make the opening bigger."

"Hurry, then!" Meg and Kerry jumped up and down. "We want to go inside, too."

They didn't even think there might be danger.

11
DARK SILVER

Glenn banged away in the tunnel, making the entrance to the cellar big enough to enter. Then his feet disappeared from sight.

"Come on," he called back. "But be careful."

Kerry went next, crawling on hands and knees. Meg was last.

The first thing Meg saw was the glow from Glenn's flashlight. Then she pulled herself into the small, musty room. Slowly she stood up.

And there at last was the Ashley silver. Her heart almost stopped.

The silver had been stored on shelves. But many of the shelves had broken down. The treasure was all tumbled in heaps on the dirt floor.

There were pitchers and trays and candlesticks. There were dozens of silver spoons. There was even a set of small steel forks with bone handles, eleven in all. Meg knew where the twelfth one was!

"The silver doesn't shine," said Kerry in a surprised voice. "It's so dark!"

"Of course it is," said Glenn. "It's been lying in this damp hole for a hundred years! It needs to be polished."

He was grinning happily. He picked up one of the pitchers and rubbed it on his sleeve. "I'll bet this was made by Paul Revere himself," he said. "It must be worth a fortune!"

Meg spoke at last. "We'd better go right away and tell Miss Clara and Miss Jenny. Won't they be happy? Let's take some things to show them."

121

She took a step forward to pick up a cup. As she did so, she tripped. She fell against one of the sagging shelves.

That's all it took to make it happen. The old timbers gave way. There was a creaking rumble, and half the ceiling seemed to fall into the cellar. With it came a shower of dirt—and a scream from Kerry.

Meg was knocked down, but not badly hurt. Kerry was safe in another corner. But Glenn was struck on the back and stunned by a heavy board. To make matters worse, he had dropped his flashlight.

Meg groped around and found it. She flashed it on the spot where the tunnel had been. To her dismay she found that it was almost covered by the cave-in. Just a glimmer of light came through a tiny hole.

Heavy timbers were wedged in front of it. She tried to move one, but it wouldn't budge.

"Are you all right, Glenn?" She turned back to the boy.

He groaned a little as he stood up. "I'll be all

122

right," he said. "My arms are numb is all. As soon as they feel better I'll try to move those boards and dig us out of here."

"How can you?" Kerry wailed. "We left the shovels outside. And nobody knows where we are."

Meg was beginning to feel a little scared herself. But she was careful not to say so. As soon as Miss Clara missed them, she would get help to find them. But how soon would that be? And how would they know where to look?

Nobody knew about the old cool cellar but them. And if the cave-in had covered their shovels—Meg didn't want to think about that.

"Let's all sit down and keep calm," she said then. "Maybe we can think of some way out. Miss Clara will call Constable Hosey. He'll send out search parties. And if we hear someone on the stairway we can all shout together. They're sure to hear us."

But Meg wasn't sure at all. Behind the rock wall, under all this dirt. . . . Would anyone hear them?

Kerry sat close to Meg. Their hands crept together for comfort. After a while Glenn stood up and tried to move the boards. But another load of dirt came sliding down. He had to give up.

"The whole place might cave in," he said gloomily. "It's all my fault that you girls are here. I shouldn't have let you come in with me. I was so crazy to find that silver I didn't think—"

"It's our fault, too, Glenn," said Meg. "Daddy has told me never to go into strange places without telling someone first."

The thought of her father made a lump come to Meg's throat. She wondered if he was still in New York, or if he was back in Washington with Uncle Hal by now.

"My folks will be worried about me," said Kerry in a muffled voice. "And if we don't get out soon, Meg, who will feed and water Chappie?"

Meg and Kerry had been riding Chappie and Traveler that day. The two horses were tied to the picket fence.

"Oh, don't worry about that, Kerry." Meg tried to make her voice bright. "Miss Clara will get someone to look after them."

"There's one good thing." Glenn sounded almost cocky. "There isn't anybody who has to worry over what happens to me. I don't *have* anybody."

"That's not so," Meg insisted. "Miss Jenny and Miss Clara would worry about you. They're awfully kind.

"Oh, let's stop this silly talk," she added. "Somebody's sure to find us soon. Let's tell stories!"

So they told stories. Glenn told all about the town he had lived in, in Ohio. And about the orphanage where he had stayed after his mother died. He told funny things to make them laugh.

They sang songs together. But their mouths got dry, and they began to feel terribly hungry.

"I wish I had a drink of water," said Kerry. "I'm so hungry I could eat a fried lizard!"

"I wish I had some of Miss Clara's pancakes," said Glenn.

Meg licked her dry lips and sighed.

Once they thought they heard noises outside. They shouted and screamed as loud as they could. But nobody came.

125

Meg lost all track of time. Glenn saved the flash-light as much as he could. It was very dark. Meg wondered sleepily if Miss Clara had called Uncle Hal to tell him she was missing. People must be looking everywhere by now.

Then she did hear a sound! It came from far off somewhere. It was the sound of a dog whining and barking. Curly was on the hill outside. Somehow, he knew they were in there.

"Everybody be quiet!"

Meg got up, her heart quick with hope. She crawled close to the spot where the boards had crashed down. There was still that tiny hole through the hill. Maybe Curly could get through it.

"Here, Curly! Here, Curly!" she called. "Please, boy—listen to Meg."

His keen ears heard her voice. He began to whim-per and bark louder than ever. If he made enough noise someone might hear him.

Then Meg realized that the little dog was pawing in the soft earth. He was trying to reach them. His whine sounded closer.

Now Kerry and Glenn were beside Meg. They added their voices to hers. "Come on, old boy!" shouted Glenn.

Meg didn't see how Curly could do it. But the brave little fellow kept digging away. And suddenly he was there!

He jumped onto Meg's legs. He licked her dirty face.

Meg was crying and laughing at the same time. She knew exactly what she was going to do.

She took her tiny sketch pad and a pencil from her pocket. Squinting in the fading light of the dim flashlight, she printed a desperate message. Just as she finished, the flashlight burned out. She could only pray that the words could be read.

> "We are trapped in an old cool cellar
> behind the wall of the witch's stair-
> way. Please help us.
>
> "Kerry, Glenn, and Meg"

In the dark, she folded it around Curly's collar and tied it with a string from her sneakers. Then she turned the little dog around and pushed him back through the tunnel he had made. He didn't want to leave them. But she cut off his return with a board. Finally they heard him digging his way back to the outside.

Meg knew that he would soon go back to the house. Miss Clara would pick him up to pat him. Then Miss Jenny would take her turn.

They would see the note.

"I only hope he hurries," said Kerry, "and that nothing happens to him on the way."

12
GLENN
COMES HOME

It seemed like many hours before they heard someone pounding on the wall of the witch's stairway. The three prisoners moved close to the old hidden door.

They shouted. "Here we are!"

The voice that answered sounded like it belonged to Constable Hosey. It was very faint. But Meg thought he said, "Hold your horses in there! We'll have you out in no time."

It took longer than that. It took work to bring the old wall tumbling down. But finally a hole was made. The rotting hidden door was unlocked, and the three weary treasure hunters were free at last.

Meg was surprised to find that it was almost morning! The first face she saw when she crawled out onto the stairway was her father's.

"I should spank you, young lady," Mr. Duncan said as he hugged his daughter. "Your Uncle Hal and I flew down from Washington. Kerry's parents, your Uncle Hal, and I have been hunting everywhere for you three. Thank heaven, you're safe! If the dog hadn't brought your note to Miss Clara—"

"Well, I just hope this adventure was worth all the worry it caused," said Uncle Hal, coming up. He, too, hugged Meg and gave one of her braids a playful tug. "Did you find that lost silver, Maggie-me-love?"

"Did we!"

Glenn Morgan was the last to come out of the cellar. His face was plastered with dirt, but he wore a big grin. He handed Uncle Hal the silver pitcher.

"There's plenty more where that came from."

"Wow!" That was all Uncle Hal could say.

"I'm hungry," cried Kerry in a loud voice. "I don't care if all the silver in the world is in that old cellar. I just want to eat."

It was much later. Everyone was in the Ashley kitchen. Kerry had called her mother and father to tell them that she was safe. The young people had washed the dirt from their hands and faces.

Now Miss Clara was making scrambled eggs and a mountain of toast for them.

And Miss Jenny, beaming like a light, was already polishing the long-lost silver. It wasn't easy, with one arm in a plaster cast. But she was doing it.

The silver lay everywhere—on the table, on the chairs, on the floor. And Constable Hosey was still bringing more in.

"What a treasure!" he said.

Uncle Hal kept picking things up and putting them down. "Most of it was made by Paul Revere himself. It's worth a king's ransom."

"What will they do with it all?" asked Kerry. She took a big, wonderful bite of scrambled egg.

"Museums all over the country will want some of it. I'm sure Miss Clara and Miss Jenny will have all the money they need when they sell it."

At that, Miss Clara looked at Miss Jenny. Miss Jenny looked at Miss Clara.

"But it isn't ours to sell," said Miss Jenny. "It really belongs to Glenn. It was his great-grandmother who hid the silver in the cellar."

"Yes," agreed Miss Clara. "And he helped Meg and Kerry find it, too. If it hadn't been for these three young people, the silver would still be in the ground."

For a moment there was silence. Then Glenn Morgan put down his fork and stood up.

"I can't take it, Miss Clara," he said. "I did come here to your house planning to take the silver if I found it. But I've changed my mind. The silver was on your land. You've been kind to me, but I'll be moving on in the morning—"

"You can't do that, Glenn." Miss Jenny was

almost in tears. "We need you. We've grown very fond of you."

"Now, just a minute." Uncle Hal put down a silver tray and went to stand beside the boy. "It seems to me as if you all have a claim to this family fortune. Why don't you share it?"

"Why not?" cried Miss Clara. "Glenn can have a home with us and help us with the chickens."

"And he can go to school in Hidden Springs. And there may be enough money for college." Miss Jenny looked almost young again.

"How about it, Glenn?" Uncle Hal put a hand on his shoulder. "You'd be a dunce to pass up an offer like that."

"I sure would, Mr. Ashley." Glenn looked proudly at the two old ladies. "Thank you, Miss Clara and Miss Jenny. I feel like I've come home at last!"

Meg smiled at Kerry. Kerry grinned back. They had done it again. They had solved a mystery a hundred years old. They had helped three fine people. Little Miss Melinda Ashley would have liked that!